Jim & Jane Become Nudist - Would You Dare to Bare? - Book 1 of the Orange Blossom Series

The Orange Blossom Nudist Resort, Volume 1

W.E. Sinful

Published by W.E. Sinful, 2015.

This is a work of fiction. Similarities to real people, places, or events are entirely coincidental.

JIM & JANE BECOME NUDIST - WOULD YOU DARE TO BARE? - BOOK 1 OF THE ORANGE BLOSSOM SERIES

First edition. February 1, 2015.

ISBN: 979-8227736048

Written by W.E. Sinful.

Table of Contents

Jim & Jane
Become Nudists
Would You Dare to Bare?
Book 1 of the
Orange Blossom Nudist Resort
Series
By W.E. Sinful

Thank you for reading

Introduction

The Orange Blossom Nudist Resort series is a fictional book dealing with the sexual adventures of singles and couples at a fictitious nudist resort. The series is not intended to depict the actual nudist lifestyle but to take readers on a sexual fantasy.

In this book, readers follow Jim and Jane's early adventures as they enter a nudist lifestyle. They start going to a topless beach, then nude beaches, and finally, the Orange Blossom Nudist Resort. They enjoy their new leisure-time activity with its sexual benefits. At first, they are afraid to tell anyone about their clothes-free adventures, but eventually, they confide in their best friend, Debbie. She is supportive and joins them for a couple of their nude beach trips. In this book, sex is steamy, but Jim and Jane remain faithful to their marriage, but **_not so much_** in the future stories.

The second book of the series is Debbie Wants to Go. In this book, Jim and Jane tell Debbie about their journey to The Orange Blossom. Their description of their latest adventure captures Debbie's erotic fantasies, and Jane invites her to join them on their next trip. Debbie eagerly agrees and does the Orange Blossom in a big way as she releases her pent-up sexual desires. Read and see if Jim's fantasies with Debbie come true.

In 'The Bare Assets Band, ' readers learn how the band that plays in the nude came to be. They started as a regular nightclub band. Still, they had to overcome their modesty when their financial needs required them to accept an offer to play at the Orange Blossom Nudist Resort. They end up doing much more than just becoming nudists...

In 'What Did You Do This Weekend?', Rachel, a co-worker of Jim's, learns that Jim and his wife Jane have a naked secret, that of being nudists. After overcoming their initial embarrassment of being discovered, Jim and Jane invite Rachel and her husband to the Orange Blossom.

These erotic fantasies have it all: Virgin sex, interracial, foursomes, voyeur, orgy, bondage, anal, striptease, nude beach, and more.
Also note: The Orange Blossom is an erotic fictional series and not intended to depict an actual or typical nudist lifestyle.

Chapter 1

Tahitian Vacation

It all started innocently enough when Jim's wife, Jane, began planning their summer vacation. Spending most of their lives in south and central Florida, they often went somewhere nearby, like the Caribbean. Other times, they would go north, to the Appalachian Mountains, to escape Florida's heat and humidity.

Jane, however, was looking for something more exotic this time. She wanted more exciting tales and photos to share with our friends and coworkers. Their same old same old was not good enough for an Instagram world.

They had saved up a little more money than usual, so they looked at Europe, Hawaii, or somewhere out west. Wherever they ended up, Jim suspected there would be a beach. For Jane, it is not a vacation without some sand and sun. Considering their budget and available vacation time, they would be able to take a couple of weeks.

After looking at many locations, Jane finally hit upon Tahiti in French Polynesia.

"Jim, Tahiti sounds like just what I'm looking for. Do you think we could afford it?"

"We probably wouldn't be taking too many side trips on an island that size, and since we will be spending most of our time at the beach, that will save a little money. It definitely sounds like an adventure, Jane. Let's run the numbers."

Jane liked the idea that they would be in a foreign country where they spoke French, which sounded romantic. She selected what looked like a lovely beachfront hotel. She wanted to relax and soak up the sun with a few side trips to explore the island and local culture.

Now, Jane was not naive. They had been to various beaches where many women wore skimpy bikinis. Some wore thong-type bottoms, and a few even went topless on one of the Caribbean islands. Thongs are generally not allowed at most Florida beaches. Still, they had seen them at South Beach in Miami, where a thong bottom was allowed, but it was not the norm. Jane did not think she would be surprised by anything Tahiti would have to throw at her.

She did not have a problem with the occasional eye candy for Jim at South Beach. She was not a prude, as she liked to wear tiny string bikinis herself so she would have minimal tan lines.

She felt more comfortable if more daring women wore skimpier attire at the beaches they visited. In that way, she figured she would not stand out or be made to feel paranoid wearing her little string bikini. She thought Tahiti would be the same.

Wrong...

Jane booked the flights and rooms for a beachfront hotel in Tahiti about a month in advance to get the best rates. They then waited patiently for their scheduled vacation to begin. After a long, agonizing flight in a cramped coach seat, they finally arrived in Tahiti and went to their hotel room to check-in. It was getting late in the evening when they arrived, so they decided to visit the nightclub in the hotel for a meal and a few drinks before visiting the beach in the morning.

They were ready for the beach after sleeping in and enjoying a leisurely breakfast. Jane wore her favorite black string bikini with a cover-up and her SFP 4 tanning lotion. Jim took his bottle of SPF 50. Jane always laughed at him, but he had no desire to test his luck with skin cancer. However, he did enjoy lying out to soak up the heat of the sun's rays. They were ready to head for the beach across from their hotel.

As soon as they stepped onto the beach, Jane was in shock. Most of the women were topless, including the women her age.

Jane quickly picked a spot and spread their towels out. They then went through the ritual of slathering on the tanning lotion. It was all Jim could do, not to stare at all the boobs. After all, Jim was a happily married man. Besides, he did not want to catch hell for staring or spring a massive boner in a public place. However, he could not help but sneak a few peeks. There were so many bold, bouncing titties on display, small ones, big ones, light ones, dark ones, firm ones, and saggy ones. As a well-endowed beauty walked by, with her breasts gently swaying in time to her steps, he had to swallow hard to keep his tongue from falling out. Better, pretend not to notice, Jim thought to himself. Not a problem, though. Jane was too busy looking for herself.

They both pretended to stare out at the ocean for a while.

Finally, Jane spoke up. "Most women my age aren't wearing tops. And some have skimpy thong-type bottoms. I'm sure you've noticed."

Now, how does a guy answer a question like that? Jim thought. It is the same as when a woman asks you if a dress makes her look fat. Jim couldn't say he did not notice, and he definitely couldn't comment on her age.

"Well..."

"Jim, I changed my mind. I want to check out more of the island."

Saved!

"You can stay here if you want to enjoy the sights."

Jim was not the sharpest tool in the shed, but he got this one. "I would rather we stick together. Let's return to our room and look at some of those brochures we picked up at the front desk."

After two days of exploring the island tourist traps, Jan found nothing else that caught her fancy. However, Jim was not the one who was going to be the first to suggest trying the beach again.

On the night of the third day, Jane realized she was starting to get a farmer's tan.

"How will I explain why I don't have an all-over tan to my friends and coworkers? I have been trying to avoid the beach because of all those topless women. However, I am going to have to swallow my pride. Just try not to stare at all the bare boobs too much. Obviously, you will enjoy this vacation a lot more than I will. You're going to owe me big time."

The next morning, they started as if they did the first day. Jane with her black bikini and SPF 4, Jim with his SPF 50.

After about an hour of lying out, Jim suggested they walk the surf. Jane sat up and looked around. There are only a couple of topless women, but they are outnumbered by several older women wearing one-piece suits.

Then she spotted two women further down the beach. Although they were much older, probably in their fifties, they strolled along bare-breasted.

"Jim, oh my God, I can't do this. Look at those two, letting it all hang out. Everyone will think I'm an old prude."

"Hell, Jane. Maybe you should give it a try."

"But all the guys will stare at me. Would you really be OK with me being half-naked?"

"The guys have a lot of other women to look at, so it wouldn't be like they're just focused on you. Look at it this way. We will be flying home in a couple of days, and we will never see any of these people again. As I see it, I get a rare chance to show off my wife's hot body and let the guys drool over what I have. It would certainly make this a vacation to remember. We just won't be able to tell anyone about it."

"Okay, but how do I get my top off without drawing too much attention? What do I do? Take my top off and simply fling it aside. That would be obvious."

"I've got an idea. Lay face down, and I will undo your top. Continue to lie that way for a while and then casually roll over like you always go topless."

"That's a dumb idea."

"You got a better one?"

With that, Jane laid down, and Jim undid her top. She then carefully slid it away while keeping her boobs on the towel. Jim got restless after about half an hour. "Are you ready to try to roll over?"

"Jim, sit up first and make sure not too many guys are hanging around."

Jim looked around and saw what seemed to be a typical crowd of beachgoers. "Eh, there are a couple of guys over to our left checking out the girls. However, they seem to be preoccupied with checking out a couple of topless teenagers wearing tiny thongs in their sight. Those girls look like they are under 18. I bet those guys could go to jail for what's on their minds."

"They sound like pervs, Jim. Are you sure it is, okay?"

"They may be perverts, but the same guys who check out 18-year-olds weren't normally interested in more mature women. Look, Jane, let us get real. You will have to wait forever for a totally deserted beach. If you are going to do this, sit up and bring your knees up to your chest; that way, you'll be partly covered. Then when you are comfortable, you can starch your legs out to expose your tits." It was as good a plan as any. Besides, Jane couldn't hide forever by lying on her belly.

After sitting up, Jane looked at the two teen girls to her left. Not only were they topless, but they were also wearing tiny G-string bottoms.

"Those girls? How do you figure they could be teenagers? Their ass cheeks are on display for the whole world to see. Surely their parents wouldn't let them run around like that?"

"I didn't look that closely, Jane. You may be right." Jim was not going to tell her he had taken a second look. He was not about to admit he had noticed how perky their breasts were, with absolutely no sag whatsoever. Nor was Jim about to confess, observing how their nipple and aureoles were not as large as the more mature females on display. He would risk getting slapped silly for checking them out. Then Jim would have to convince Jane that her breasts looked just as tasty. He would then risk getting smacked a second time when bumbling through a clumsy expression of male appreciation. In truth, he felt Jane did have beautiful boobs. Although not huge, they had kept a youthful firmness.

After a few minutes, Jane felt more comfortable. She decided it was time to get up and walk the beach. They strolled down to the water and turned to the right, away from the crowd of potential oglers. Jim took his usual position closer to the edge of the water. That way, Jane, who was shorter, would be at about eye level with Jim. Jane usually liked that, but not today.

"Honey, switch sides with me. That way, you'll be between most of the sunbathers and me. That way, you'll be partly hidden by your body."

"Still feeling shy, gorgeous? There's no reason you should."

"I know it won't do much good, but it still will make me feel a little better."

It was a warm day, as most days were in Tahiti. Jane's skin was already glowing, beginning to collect a faint sheen of sweat. Jim slipped his arm around her waist and felt the delicious heat of two nearly naked bodies in contact.

"You know what, Jim? This really feels nice. Normally, my top pushes my boobs against my body, making little pools of sweat collect on the underside of my titties."

Jim watched a tiny drop of moisture run down between her bouncing globes before vanishing. He would have loved to chase it with his tongue.

"I also like how my boobs gently sway as I walk; it feels very free and even a little erotic." Jane took Jim by the hand and squeezed just his fingertips. "We may have to go back to our room pretty soon to take care of a burning desire I'm starting to develop."

"Same here. You're so hot without a top that I'm getting a semi," Jim said. "These swim trunks aren't as baggy as when I put them on in the morning."

"Are you sure you don't have a problem with my boobs hanging out like this in front of the other men?"

"Hell no, I trust you're not going to run off with any of them. Besides, I like showing off my hot wife, and most men with good-looking wives would do the same if they got the chance. However, if you continue to heat me up, that little rise you gave me will be a bigger problem. You know the old saying, the angle of the dangle is equal to the heat of the meat."

They began approaching a hot-looking, topless woman in the surf as they walked. She had her back to us, but we could tell she was about Jane's age and size. Her boobs, waist, and hips were all about the same as Jane's. The big difference was that she was wearing a black G-string bottom. It had strings tied off in bows at the sides of her hips, like those on Jane's suit. Instead of attaching to a triangular patch of cloth covering her butt, they continued around her waist to a silver ring at the top of her butt crack. A third string then led down from the ring and disappeared between the cheeks of her ass, presumably attaching to the small triangular piece of cloth covering her crotch in front. Her butt cheeks were on full display. Jim just wanted to reach out and grab a cheek in each hand. Oh, Jim knew they would have to return to their room soon. The woman's G-string was black, his wife's favorite color. Jane could not help but make the same comparison Jim was making.

"You think I would ever dare to wear a thong like that? Besides having an all-over tan on my boobs, I would have a tanned butt as well."

"As I said before, Jane, we'll never see any of these people again. I say, go for it!"

"Are you ready to shop?" For the first time, on their vacation, she really smiled.

"Fuck, yeah!"

They returned to their beach towels, only long enough to get dressed and head back. As Jane lifted her arms to tie her top on, Jim could not keep his eyes off her beautiful tits.

By the time they got to their room, Jim's cock was throbbing; he was in agony as it strained against the confines of his trunks, with all those lush naked boobs at the beach! Including his wife's. Especially his wife's!

Jane entered first, and Jim closed the door behind them and immediately began to slide his swimsuit down past his hips. This allowed his dick to spring free. As the trunks fell to his ankles, Jim stepped forward in a continuous walking motion and was instantly stark naked. Scrambled up from behind, Jane was caught by surprise as Jim slammed into her backside. Jane could feel Jim's rigid cock push against the silky fabric covering her butt. At the same time, Jim reached around to cup her firm tits through her bikini top, one in each hand.

Jim squeezed her firm tits while kissing the nape of her neck, shoulders, and the shell of her delicate ears.

"Oh!" Jane moaned as she began humping herself back against his cock. Jane then reached down to rub her pussy through her swimsuit. Her thighs spread slightly to let her fingers do their work.

After a moment, Jane broke loose from his hands, gripping her tits, and turned around to face Jim. Her eyes were glassy with passion. Putting her arms around him, she gave him an endless soul kiss as her tongue went deep to explore the inner deeps of his mouth.

It was time. Jim slid his fingers under the bottom of her bikini top and raised it over her boobs, causing them to tumble free.

"Mmmm yessss," her voice barely moaned as his hands closed around her naked tits to rub her sensitive nipples.

"I've been staring at your gorgeous tits all day and can't take it any longer," Jim said. He then grabbed ahold of her bare boobies so that he could run his tongue around her super-sensitive nipples. Yes, fuck, yes. Jim began to suck. His tongue flickered over her right nipple and then the left, darting back and forth between them as Jane kept moaning and squirming.

He gently pushed her onto the bed as his hands slid to Jane's bikini panties. The crotch of her bikini was soaked entirely through due to her flowing pussy juices. It was evident from the spreading dark patch that she was as turned on as Jim. Jim tugged down the top of her bikini bottom to reveal the top of her little copper-colored cunt bush. She kept it neatly trimmed in a narrow landing strip pattern—and landing his hard dick in that hot cunt below was all that was on Jim's mind. He pulled the bottoms the rest of the way off as Jane opened her thighs to expose the soaking-wet pink interior of her pussy.

Jim ran his fingers across her slippery love mound before inserting two fingers into the wet inviting slit. The folds of her cunt lips pressed against his exploring fingers as he spread the crack of her pussy wide open to get to her clit. Her love nubbin was huge and swollen, an open invitation. Jim stroked it repeatedly, and she cried out in pleasure whenever he touched her there.

As a tease, he shifted his attention from her love button to her pink tunnel. His index and middle fingers began to slide inside her hot, drippy cunt in a series of deep, eager strokes. The only reason he removed his hand was, so he could use his tongue to stroke up and down Jane's cunt. He could taste her wetness, tangy and hot, oozing into his mouth and coating his tongue as he worked it up and down between her lower lips. Jane's clitoris was a bud of protruding hardness at the top of her cunt, beckoning Jim to lash at it repeatedly with the tip of his tongue.

"Mmmm, honey, I love that." She slid her hands up to her tits to squeeze them and roll the nipples between her fingers as he ate her out. "Yes... Yes. Eat my pussy!"

Jim climbed between her thighs while keeping his tongue planted in her twat. He could feel the muscles of her cunt tightening against his face as if she were trying to trap his tongue deep inside her pussy.

"Oh, Jim... Eat me!" Jane clutched at the back of his head to keep his face pressed against her cunt.

She wrapped her thighs around his neck to better grind her oozing slit into his face. Her wet pussy humped against his tongue again and again. He shoved his oral digit up inside her love tunnel to make her moan. She was already loud, but he knew he could make her scream louder.

He placed his hands on the cheeks of her ass to pull her pussy harder against his mouth and tongue. He was now licking her pussy in long strokes from her puckered pink asshole to the shiny-wet folds around her clit. Her juices gushed over his face, and the raunchy smell of female excitement turned him on even more. He concentrated on her clit, stroking it rapidly up and down. Jane squirmed on the bed, clawing at the back of his scalp, spreading her thighs further and further apart, hammering his mouth against her pussy. Her body tensed. Oh yeah, she was definitely screaming now.

"Oh, shit... I am coming! I'm coming!" She screamed as she lifted her ass off the bed. She arched her back as she came with a savage intensity that pressed her orgasming twat firmly against his face. Her sopping wet cunt juices smeared his face and began to run down her ass cheeks and onto the bed. Jim's head rocked back with each spasm while his tongue kept stabbing in and out of her cunt.

"I'm coming again... I'm coming again..."

He let her come a few more seconds and then stopped. Prying her legs open, he slipped his face out of her gripping thighs. Standing boldly, he openly began to massage his throbbing cock.

"I can't stand this anymore. I have been imagining me was sliding my dick into your hot wet pussy all afternoon as I watched you parade around. Your boobs were bouncing around all over the place. And all those drooling guys watching you have been an absolute turn-on for me!"

"I've been horny as hell too. I wanted you to fuck me all afternoon." Jane shuddered with lust. "So quit dicking around and use that dick of yours!"

Jim forcibly grabbed her ankles to spread her like a wishbone and then lunged forward to jab his swollen prick savagely into her waiting cunt. He watched intently as his cock plunged into her gaping wet hole. Her cunt lips gobbled the length of his shaft until their bellies were pressed so tightly together his balls would slap against her ass cheeks.

The powerful internal muscles of her cunt sucked his cock even further inside her. He then quickly began thrusting in and out of her slippery depths. He let go of her ankles and fell forward, holding her on the bed by her shoulders. She raised her head to meet him, and their tongues intertwined in a lustful kiss.

Arching her back and fucking upwards, Jane screamed. "Fuck, Jim, God, FUCK ... I'm coming again." Her cunt clutched his dick even tighter.

It took a while for Jane to come down from her orgasm. However, when she did, Jim pulled her thighs open more. Her pussy was all the more vulnerable and exposed to his wild hammering. Her fluttering pink hole lay wide open like a target pierced to the hilt by the shaft of a skydiving dick.

"Oh, fuck!" She arched her back again. Her hips bucked. She came yet another time again and maybe even again. She could not seem to stop. Jim could not hold out any longer. It was his turn. He moaned and then shouted as his sperm exploded into the hot wet depths of her cunt. Her vibrating love tunnel was like a soft velvety hand gripping around his cock, urging him to keep coming as it sucked his dick dry. He spasmed endlessly as her muscular pussy sucked a gallon of cum out of his dick, filling and overflowing her twitching love tunnel.

After Jim's orgasm subsided, he rolled off her and onto his back. As he turned, his cum-coated dick pulled out of her twat and made a plopping sound slapping against his belly. It was one of the most intense orgasms of his life. Afterward, they lay there on the bed for a while, satisfied and exhausted.

Then Jane rolled over on Jim, put one knee between his legs, and wrapped her arms around him. As she kissed him, cum and pussy juices flowed out of her hot dripping cunt, to flood the bed. They drowsed off a little, neither one giving a damn about the fucking wet spot.

At some point, he felt her lips on his mouth and then on his ear. "That was hot. I must have come at least a half-dozen times." She said after breaking off the kiss. "Now, let's get dressed and go shopping."

As they got up, Jane looked back at the cum and pussy drippings smeared all over the bed. "We'll have to clean that mess up later. Right now, I just want to go."

Neither of them was in the mood for a lengthy shopping trip. Jane headed for the gift shop directly across from the hotel and went straight to a rack of G-string bikinis. She picked out a black one her size, similar to the one worn by the lady on the beach—except it had a gold ring with a few rhinestones around the edge.

"You must have seen these earlier since you went right to this rack," Jim said.

Jane flushed a little. "Yes, I did. I thought I could not wear something like this in public without getting arrested. I never dreamed you would let me do it, even if it was legal. But when I saw the lady on the beach, I knew I wanted it. And then you said to go for it..."

"The gold accent makes this one look more expensive than hers. Are you ready to try it on?"

Jane went back into the dressing room. She returned a few minutes later with a big smile and the thong in her hand.

"I tried it on, and it fits perfectly. I would come out and show you, but I was a little embarrassed to model it in the store. You'll just have to wait until we get to the beach to see me in it."

"Well then, let's pay up and get going."

They changed into beachwear in their hotel room, and Jane wasted no time. She picked out a tight-fitting tee shirt to use as a beach cover-up and headed straight for the bathroom with the G-string bottoms in hand.

She emerged in a few minutes, looking as sexy as hell. Her long wavy red hair flowing down her back emphasized how her tits strained against the material of her tight-fitting shirt. Her large, engorged nipples were clearly outlined beneath the fabric. It was apparent she did not have a bikini top underneath.

The tee stopped short of her crotch to expose the bottom of the black G-string, an open invitation to check out her itty-bitty bikini. Her tits swayed as she moved. She did a slow pirouette so Jim could enjoy every angle. The under-curve of Jane's two bare ass cheeks was clearly visible beneath the hem of the brief cover-up. From behind, she looked naked under the shirt except for the outline of the tiny G-string around her waist.

"Take the tee shirt off so I can see the full effect of that little G-string."

"You'll have to wait until we get to the beach." She wore a sly smirk.

They worked their way across the crowded beach, thinking it did not seem this busy a couple of hours ago, as Jane looked for the best place to spread their blankets. She felt nervous again but finally picked a reasonably secluded spot, about halfway down the beach from the water's edge. She had no intention of going into the water. Her little bikini was strictly for catching the attention of ogling males and jealous females. One good-sized wave would mean she would be in big trouble, but she did want to get a few gawkers, just not too many.

As they spread their blankets out, several pairs of eyes were already probing Jane with more than casual interest. She was not yet daring enough to bend over to fix the corners, so she moved the fabric around with her toes. Jim anchored them with their flip-flops and beach bag. After a few minutes of fussing with the beach blanket, she had nothing left to do but take off her shirt.

Jim sat down with Jane, still standing, and lifted his gaze to the appropriate spot.

"Are you ready?" She gripped the bottom edge of her shirt and raised it over her head.

Several guys were watching Jane. Both Jane and Jim saw them and acted as if they did not notice them staring. First, she raised the bottom of the shirt to just under her tits and looked down at Jim for approval. He smiled, and Jane took the hint, quickly pulling the shirt off over her head, a gesture that allowed her barely constrained tits to pop free in Jim's direction. After combing her fingers through her hair to get the tangles, she slowly made a single pirouette. On tiptoe, she turned around once to ensure Jim got a good view of her ass before she stopped and faced him again. Her petite figure gave her a very youthful appearance.

"Do you like it?"

"Hell yeah!"

His wife was standing in front of him in public for all to see. For all intent and purpose, she was completely naked except for the small triangle of black cloth covering her pussy. Several of the guys nearby could not look away from the sexy display. Jane noticed, but she did not seem to mind.

Jim was enjoying the envious stares himself. He knew he would be able to screw his hot babe's brains out later, and all the gawkers would get were a few minutes of drool time.

"Let's go walk the beach, Jim. I want to show this little thing off."

"Okay, but try not to shake that gorgeous ass of yours too much, or I'll shoot my load at a moment's notice."

They strolled along the beach. Jane was getting a lot of attention, and she knew it and seemed to enjoy it as much as the watchers did. Jim had consistently told Jane what a smoking body she had, and Jane would always brush the comment off, saying that he was trying to butter her up to get into her pants. All this attention from the other guys made her realize that it was not just Jim saying it; they thought the same thing.

After she paraded around for a while, they laid out until it was getting close to dinnertime. They were both getting a little hungry and decided it was time to go to their room, change clothes, and get a bite.

Back in the room, Jane removed her cover-up and flung it on the bed as Jim peeled off his trunks. With her back towards him, she slid down her thong. When it reached her ankles, she bent over and started to step out of it.

Jim could not control himself any longer. He dropped to his knees behind her and buried his face in that delicious-looking ass.

"Hey!!!" Jane let out a surprised yelp as he placed one hand on her bare butt cheeks and pushed them onto the bed.

Jim gently pulled her legs apart so that he could get his face further into her ass. He stuck his tongue into her cunt from behind and ran it back to her asshole several times. Her cunt was sopping wet with pussy juices. Her winking pucker was now thoroughly juiced up with pussy juice and saliva, so he stuck his tongue up into her asshole as far as he could.

Jane let out a satisfying "Ahh..." as he began to fuck her tiny butthole with his tongue.

By this time, Jim had another raging hard-on. He felt her pussy with his hand and gently stuck a thumb up her cunt. Her juices gushed over his hand and onto the bed.

"Jim, I can't take it any longer. Stick your hard cock up my pussy right now!"

Jim stood up slightly, took his cock in hand, and guided it into that dripping snatch to enter her from behind, doggy style. He slid in with ease, going all the way. Grabbing her ass, he started pumping in and out. After a few short thrusts, Jane's body stiffened, and her pussy squeezed around his dick as she rushed toward orgasm.

"I'm coming ... I'm coming!"

Feeling her intense orgasm was more than Jim could stand, and he could no longer hold back. His balls began to blast their load as he pumped what seemed like a gallon of cum into her hot pussy. No sooner had he finished than Jane started to come a second time.

After she finished, Jim pulled out and collapsed in the center of the bed, and Jane crawled close beside him. For the moment, they were both too tired to stand, much less clean up. Cum, pussy juice, and saliva drooled from her dripping cunt onto the bedspread.

They were not sure how long they cuddled, but Jane remembered she was hungry at some point. "We really should get cleaned up for dinner. This bed is shameful, with two huge cum stains on the linens in five hours. What the fuck will the housekeeper think?"

"She'll think it's a good thing that Americans tip well. Besides, we'll never see her again."

That evening, after dinner and another trip to the beach, they repeated their sexcapades once more. After three fucks in one day, Jane's pussy was sore, and Jim's balls were drained. However, they did not let up, as they only had a few days left in Tahiti. For the rest of the vacation, they would go to the beach, where Jane would flaunt her stuff; they would get horny, return to their room, fuck like bunnies, and then repeat. They were screwing three or four times a day, more than they did on their honeymoon.

On the last day at the beach, Jane decided she wanted some personal photos for souvenirs. Therefore, they found a secluded cove where Jim used a digital camera to take some pictures of Jane topless in her tiny G-string bikini. He grabbed several shots of her walking along the surf's edge. In some, she walked toward Jim to show off her gorgeous bare boobs. In others, she walked away to show off her exposed derriere, dressed only in the small strings from the G-string wrapped around her waist and disappeared down the crack of her ass. These rear views gave little indication that she was not fully nude.

"Jane, I'd like to have a couple of shots of you and me together." A young guy was not too far away, about twenty feet from the shoreline. He was probably in his late teens and was trying to act as if he was not watching. They both knew better.

"Do you think I can ask him to take some pictures of us?" Jim said, pointing to the guy.

"Sure," Jane said with an evil twinkle in her eye and a devious smile on her lips. Jane had changed so much from being a blushing prude a few days ago.

"Hey, buddy. Do you think you could take a couple of shots of my wife and me?"

"Oh... OK." He blinked, trying to look as if he had not been paying attention all along. Jim handed him the camera and walked back down to the water's edge by his wife. First, they turned toward the cameraman with their backs to the ocean. Jim stood behind Jane, slightly off to her right, with his left hand over her left shoulder. Jim purposely placed his wrist on the very top of her shoulder. This allowed his hand to dangle down. It was as if he was about to grab her exposed tit at any moment.

The young man took a couple of shots from his position halfway up the beach.

"You seem a little far away." Jane waved him to come closer and smiled.

"Come closer so you can get a better shot."

He hesitated. From the growing bulge in his trunks, it was apparent to both that the kid was getting turned on by Jane's use of the term 'closer shot.' That phrase had multiple meanings. Not only would he get a better camera shot, but also, he would get a better view of the hot boobs his eyes had locked onto. One could develop a third meaning of the phrase and how it might affect the fluids collecting in his balls.

"It's okay, baby," Jane said. "We won't bite."

He blushed, but if good manners required him to get close to Jane's naked ta-tas, how could a red-blooded man refuse? Therefore, he came forward to grab a few more snaps. Jane turned towards Jim as she seductively adjusted her G-string, first by pulling it away from her crotch and then letting her thumbs slide along the side strings to raise them on her hips.

When she moved in closer, she rotated her ass more toward him. Her tits rubbed against the side of Jim's chest, and her crotch bumped against his leg. The young guy could not see the front of her G-string bottom, only her bare hip and butt cheek. From his viewpoint, she would have looked utterly naked except for the delicate string around her waist. His raging hard-on pushed out the front of his trunks. He looked embarrassed, if not in out-and-out pain.

After Jane had thoroughly enjoyed torturing him, she took their camera back. "Thanks, man." She spoke.

He walked away quickly without a word, adjusting his trunks as he did.

"How long do you think before that poor boy jacks off?" Jane giggled. "Think he'll make it back to his hotel room?"

"He'll be lucky to make it to the other side of that palm tree," Jim said.

"This is payback for all the times in high school when my boyfriend couldn't finish what he started, and I had to finger my wet pussy in the girl's room," Jane said as she hooked her arm in Jim's. "This time, I intend to take my guy back to my room and fuck his brains out."

"Oh, the joy of being brainless," Jim said. "I can't wait."

By the end of the vacation, Jane's pussy and Jim's dick were as sore as they had been on their honeymoon.

Chapter 2

Got to Tell Someone!

Jane and Jim both agreed that Tahiti had been the most magnificent trip ever and that they would have to make it again soon. There was one big problem ... cost. They could not afford to go to Tahiti every vacation. Besides, waiting a whole year seemed like an unbearable prospect, even if they had unlimited funds.

Another problem was what to tell their friends, family, and coworkers. They did not have many photos, at least not that they were willing to share. Besides, they, sure as shit, could not tell them about Jane going topless in her ass-baring G-string.

Jim was hammered with questions no sooner than he had returned to work Monday morning.

Betty, the Finance Manager, who had an office directly across from his, was the first to ask about his vacation. "So, Jim, how was Tahiti? Tell me everything."

"It was great." He said, trying to keep it short and sweet.

"What did you do?" Betty asked him as her two assistants, Beth and Rachel, crowded around.

"We checked out the sights on the island, but mostly, we hung out at the beach. Just chilling, you know." Jim said.

"So, how did it go around here?" He said, trying to change the subject.

"I want to see the pictures," Rachel said.

"Erm, uh..." Why hadn't he prepared a better story, Jim thought to himself.

Beth giggled. "Let me guess. The topless beach bunnies there wouldn't let you take their photo."

That caught the attention of Big Ears, Mike, "Yeah, I heard at some of those island locations the girls go topless. You got to have some pictures?"

Great! He had a crowd of coworkers around him. He was never this fucking popular when he came back from Fort Myers.

Beth turned on Mike. "Yeah, you'd get off on that, you pervert."

"I always wondered what it would be like to go topless but never had the nerve," Betty said. "Isn't there a beach over by the Cape that's fully nude, both guys and gals?"

"I heard that too," Rachel said. "But my husband would have kittens if I said I wanted to go to a nude beach. Hell, I'd be too embarrassed anyway."

"Your husband is so controlling," Betty said. "I divorced Dan, my first husband, over control issues, and now I am fighting with Bob over the same damn thing. Rachel, you are young, have a killer figure, and nothing to be embarrassed about. If you want to go to a topless beach, you should stand up for yourself and go. Now, this chunky, over-the-hill body with saggy tits." She pointed at herself. "That's something to be embarrassed about."

"You're all a bunch of perverts. I have to get back to work." Beth said and walked away.

"I need to get to work, too," Jim said, appreciating the convenient out Beth had given him. "I'm sure I have a ton of emails to go through."

For the rest of the day, he avoided talking about his vacation.

When he got home, he told Jane about his day. She said the same thing happened at her job.

They were just as skittish with family and friends.

They were dying to tell someone about their spectacular vacation but did not know whom to trust. However, Jim and Jane just had to tell somebody. Jane finally decided to confide in her best friend, Debbie. They knew she would not take the opportunity to blast their secret to the entire world.

The next time Debbie was over at their house, Jane told her about the topless women at the beach.

"At first, I was put off by it. Then, I decided to give it a try with Jim's blessing. You'd be amazed at how free I felt going without a top."

Debbie listened intently. "That's so hot. I bet you had unbelievable sex that night!"

"Aw... we didn't wait that long," Jane said.

"Tell me more. You must have gone to the beach more than once."

"Well..." Jane's naughty smile spread from ear to ear. "After my first topless adventure, we went out that very afternoon so that I could buy a tiny G-string bikini bottom like the other women wore."

"No way, that's fucking bold," Debbie said. "I wish John would let me do something like that."

"Let me go and get it. I'll be happy to show you." Jane sprinted to their bedroom and returned a few seconds later with a grin on her face. She appeared to be empty-handed and grinned even more when she opened her clutched hand in front of Debbie to reveal the tiny G-string.

"Shit!!" Debbie's eyes and mouth went wide.

"Mind if I show her a couple of photos, Jim?"

"No. Go right ahead." He spoke.

You would have thought Debbie's tongue would fall out of her mouth when Jane showed her the photos taken by the young guy at the beach. "I gave that guy a boner to remember," Jane said, and they all laughed.

"I'm so envious of you two. I suggested something similar to John about a year ago. He immediately shot me down and said it sounded perverted. Things were a little slow in the romance department, and I thought something like that would be just the thing to spice it up. John is a missionary kind of guy who thinks nudity or any kind of oral foreplay is dirty."

"Well, Debbie, you won't be getting jealous of us repeating our Tahiti adventure anytime soon. It is just too expensive."

Debbie looked wistful. "Before John more or less called me a slut, I had looked up topless beaches in the Caribbean, which is a little more in our budget. I also checked Florida. Did you know there are several clothing-optional beaches right here in Florida? There are also several private resorts where you can go fully nude."

"I don't know about that full naked thing, Debbie," Jane said.

"The Internet said they were clothing optional. Some people would be fully naked, but not everybody. Besides, where else are you going to be able to wear that little bikini? You'll get arrested for indecent exposure wearing that thing on most beaches around here."

Jane looked at Jim. "Jim, I'm going to look into those places. We so enjoyed our time in Tahiti, but it is fucking expensive. We can't afford to go even once a year, but someplace local, where we could go every weekend, would be great."

Jim thought Debbie might be a bad influence on his wife but had to admit he appreciated her thoughts, and so did Jane. Jane spent the next several days searching the Internet to see what she could find. It turned out that they had a lot of choices. She found only one legal clothing-optional beach in Florida. Still, there were a couple of unauthorized beaches that the cops more or less ignored. There were also a surprising number of resorts. The official clothing-optional beach was Haulover Beach down in Miami.

"There are a lot of pictures of Haulover on the Internet," Jane said. "But it looks like most people go nude there, and I don't know if I'm ready for that. Besides, it also looks like it gets really crowded."

She opened another tab on her laptop. "But check out this one. It's an unauthorized beach north of the space center in a national park. On the first several beaches, swimsuits are required, and the last one is clothing optional. Many of the women opt to go topless, and some go fully nude, and it doesn't sound as if it gets as crowded as the one in Miami."

"It's about an hour away. Do you think we can check it out on Saturday, honey?" She was too excited to give Jim time to answer. "We can pack a small cooler with water and snacks. We can go to the first beach and see what it is like. If it feels right, we can go further on."

"Well, it sounds like you have thought it all out."

It was breezy when they got up on Saturday. The forecast was for sun and a high of 87 when they headed out well before noon.

The first surprise was the park entrance fee. The only access to the beach road was from the south end of the park, where they had to pass through a toll booth. After reading all the signs posted with a long list of rules, they were both a little nervous, knowing they would soon be face-to-face with a park ranger.

"You think it's obvious we're coming here to check out the nude beach, Jim?"

"How the fuck would I know? Act natural. Say we're going fishing."

"Okay, but it might be obvious we do not have fishing gear in this little car," Jane replied.

"Well, it is a little late to back out now," Jim said. He then put down his window and handed the elderly male attendant a twenty, trying not to make any more eye contact than necessary. He got the change and quickly drove off.

"Do you think he knew?" Jane asked him. "Do you think he suspected something? Do you think he visualized us without clothes on?"

"Oh well. We'll probably never see that guy again." They both said it in unison.

They stopped at the first beach parking lot to check things out. Bathing suits, tops, and bottoms were required here. The lot had about 20 cars in it and probably 50 empty spaces. They could also see the NASA launch pads to their right as they walked up and over the beach dune crossover.

"Wow. This was a great find already," Jim said. "It's a beautiful beach with hardly any people, and it looks like a great place for walking along the surf and collecting shells."

"The Internet said this was a beautiful beach, and they were right." Jane seemed encouraged. "There's supposed to be thirteen beach parking lots and one lot for accessing the lagoon behind us. Let's go up to the next lot."

They drove north along the beach access road. Each successive parking lot had fewer and fewer cars, and the tenth parking lot was empty.

"Jim, can you believe there are no cars here on such a beautiful day? Let's check it out."

They parked and crossed over the dune. Once on the beach, Jim and Jane looked left and right, and no one was in sight.

"The only thing I can figure is that it's a long drive to get here, and not many people want to make the trip," Jim said. "We left the toll booth over half an hour ago. Do you think there will be anyone at the last beach?"

"Don't know, honey. The only thing to do is drive on, as I'm becoming more curious."

They passed by another empty parking lot and then came to a lot where they finally saw some cars. It looked to be about half full.

"Jim, let's stop here a minute. This is the last beach where bathing suits are required, and I want to look around before we approach the beach where I can go topless."

It was a strange vibe. The parking lot was half-full, but there was no one walking around.

They walked up the dune crossover and looked out at the beach. Again, no one was in sight.

"Is this place possessed by zombies or something?" Jane asked Jim, giving him a nervous look. "Where is everybody?"

"Maybe they're fishing on the lagoon behind us?" Jim shrugged. "The question is, do we continue to head up the road to the last parking lot or do the smart thing and speed home as fast as we can?"

"We made it this far, Jim. We already paid, and I need to check it out."

"Okay. But I hope zombies don't attack us."

They got back in their car. As they drove, they passed a lone male walking along the side of the road—then a second male, a couple hundred feet ahead.

"That's strange." Jane locked her car door.

They spotted the last parking lot, and the mystery was solved, as it was completely full. There are plenty of people milling around, all wearing conventional bathing suits. A couple of women stood by the edge of the parking lot with beach umbrellas, coolers, and big straw beach bags. The last guy they had passed on the road walked up to one of them. The other woman was probably waiting for the first guy.

"Now I got it," Jane said. "There were no open parking spots, just multiple signs warning you not to park on the grass if you didn't want your vehicle to get towed. Guys must drop off their wives or girlfriends with their stuff before driving back to the previous lot. There were other signs posted, too."

"No Nudity Allowed." Jane read the message aloud with some disgust. "I guess it's just a regular beach."

"I doubt that, Jane. There has got to be something going on. Why would everybody pass up all those beautiful, uncrowded beaches to come here?"

"I don't know, Jim. Let's find out."

"Do you want me to drop you off here so you don't have to walk so far?"

"No, I'm not comfortable about the whole situation just yet. Besides, we did not bring that much stuff. I'll come with you."

They proceeded to park at the previous lot and walked back. When they arrived at the last lot, they followed another couple up the dune crossover. They kept thinking it looked like a regular beach. They realized they were no longer in Kansas when they reached the top.

Off to their left was a canopy. A man and a woman sat in beach chairs at a table beneath it. It was pretty ordinary except for the fact that they were totally nude! They were talking to another couple with their backs to them, also naked.

Behind them, further along the beach, there were more beachgoers of all ages, shapes, and sizes. A few ladies had tops and bottoms on, some were topless, and many others were fully nude. There were also an equal number of men, most fully naked.

To their right, it was a totally different world. Several fully clothed guys were surf fishing, for all the world, as if nothing unusual was going on.

"It's your choice, Jane. Go to the right with the surf fishers and look like a couple of gawkers, or go left to mingle with the cool kids?"

"Just follow that couple in front of us who turned left and act as if we come here all the time."

They walked past the nude people at the canopy. Soon, Jane found a beautiful open area, reasonably far from the surf and close to the dune.

Jane found what she felt was the right spot. They laid their blankets down and sat looking out at the ocean. Of course, Jim did a little girl watching but tried not to make it too noticeable. There were a lot of hot bodies to look at, too. Maybe hot girls are more likely to take their clothes off. In any case, about half were topless, and the other half were fully nude. Some of the women had complete wax jobs on their pussies. Some had landing strips like Jane. Still, others had fuller bushes in a classic triangle shape.

Jim glanced at his wife. No wonder Jane did not catch him looking; she was too busy gawking at the guys. Two nude couples stood talking not too far from them. The guy facing them had a fully shaved pubic area, probably to draw attention to the fact he was hung like a horse. Even when limp, his dick hung down at least eight inches and was bigger around than Jim's was when he was hard.

"What are you looking at, honey?" Jim asked.

She smiled. "Not the fucking ocean, that's for sure."

Why did he ask? Jim thought to himself.

"When we were in Tahiti, I enjoyed the freedom of going topless. But the eye candy was for you, wasn't it?"

Uh, no, now Jane was starting to expound, Jim thought. "Here, it's my turn to get an eyeful. I never saw a guy with shaved balls before. Going down on him would be fun without any hair in the way. I keep picturing myself licking his big stick like a giant lollipop. I would pay special attention to its underside and take the time to suck one of his bare balls into my mouth. I cannot wait until he turns around. It looks like he has a tight little ass to grab onto as I go down on him. My pussy's getting wet. If I don't watch it, I'll get an obvious damp spot in the crotch of my bathing suit."

Jim thought that was quite a speech as he sat a little stunned by the explicit details of his wife's oral fantasy.

"How about you, hon?" Jane asked, tearing her eyes off Mr. Shaved Balls long enough to give him a look of amusement. "I'm sure you checked out the two nude girls the guys brought along. The girls both look super-hot. And I'm sure you didn't miss the piercings in the lips of the one with a waxed pussy."

"I might have noticed something like that. But fuck me. I'm trying not to stare."

"Jim, that's because you know that if you check the girls out too closely, you will get an obvious hard-on."

Jim's once-baggy swim trunks were already getting a little tighter in front. What could he say?

Jane began to feel around for the knot at the back of her string bikini. "Well, I came here to go topless." The top fell off, and her boobs tumbled free.

"It feels good to let the girls breathe." She spoke. She ran her hands along the underside of her boobs, lifting them slightly. Her nipples went hard.

"There's a sight you don't see every day at the beach." Jane pointed out at the ocean. "Two guys out there surfing in the buff. It looks like they got good ones."

"You're not talking about the waves they're riding, are you?"

"Duh, I think I am going to like this beach," Jane said as a man and woman walked by, wearing swimsuits.

"Look at those two gawkers checking out the nude people." Jane snorted. "Tourists, aren't they?"

"Why do you say that, Jane?

"It's how they hold their heads high, steady, and always facing forward. They try to pretend they are not staring at the people around them. Nevertheless, their shifty eyes give them away, darting from side to side. Besides, they are still wearing their swimsuits and are coming from the parking area empty-handed. If they plan to spend time here, they would be carrying towels, water, or something. They obviously did not plan to stay very long and just wanted to look. But not participate. Creepy."

"Had you not noticed, Jane, I still have my swim trunks on? Do you think I look like a gawker? Be honest."

"Well, Jim, haven't you noticed that if the female is nude or topless, the guy with her is always nude? It's your choice. Be a gawker or be a participant."

She was right, Jim thought. It was not really in the spirit of things to enjoy gawking at everybody else while he kept his trunks on. Jim started to slide them down but had to figure out how to get them past his butt without standing up and drawing attention to himself. He decided to rock from side to side to ease them past his butt and over his knees, making his private parts not so private.

That brought him to his next problem. Not only were his privates fully exposed to the public, but they were also exposed to the sun. Any overexposure down there would be fast and painful.

"Do you feel like you fit in better, Jim?"

"I do like the feel of the cool breeze. But how do I apply suntan lotion around my dick and balls without looking like a pervert? It would be really awful if I got a hard-on. But it would be even worse to get a bad burn down there."

"Do you want me to do it for you?" Her chuckle was downright dirty.

"That won't solve anything," Jim said, reaching for the lotion. As he applied it, he did his best to think about other things.

"Jane, you may as well take off your bottoms too. That way, we look like a couple of regular pros."

"Our tan lines will make us stand out like a couple of white-tail deer. So, if you do not mind, I will. The sooner I get them off, the sooner I can start working on an all-over tan." Jane's bottoms were off in a flash, revealing her trimmed bush with its alluring slit below.

As they lay out, soaking up the sun's rays, they soon heard what sounded like a motorbike. They saw a female lifeguard in a one-piece bathing suit ride by on a four-wheeler, looking straight ahead as she drove.

"There's a job to have," Jane said. "I'd probably get into trouble, as I would be too tempted to take off my swimsuit and join in the fun. I guess that warning sign in the parking lot is bullshit, as she just cruised right by everyone."

They were starting to get comfortable being nude in public. That is when Jane decided they should go for a walk to check the rest of the beach out and stood up as casually as possible. They walked down to the water and turned north when they reached the point where the surf lapped at their feet.

As they strolled, they passed several other nude couples, some sunbathing, and others walking the other way. Both were careful not to stare. Jim, in particular, did not want to get a woody. He could not help but get a little excited, as Jane was so hot walking beside him with the sun in her hair and not a stitch of clothing on her curvy body. He could see every beautiful inch of her... an absolute turn-on. Jane's undulating tits, swaying ass, and the glistening of her succulent pussy drove him crazy. Then, they began to approach an area with a bunch of nude guys sitting in pairs.

"Watch out for those creeps," Jim said. "They might be naked, but they're here to gawk. There isn't a single woman with any of them."

Jane cracked up laughing. "Baby, I'm not the one who has to worry about those boys. If they're checking out anybody, it's you because... they're gay." With that, any pretext of an erection disappeared, and Jim's butt cheeks tightened up.

After they passed the guys, the beach became noticeably less populated. There were a few straight couples, but not very many. In fact, there were fewer and fewer people of any kind. Soon, they were virtually alone.

"Jane, the last people we passed are so far away I can barely make them out. Do we have to worry about walking up to a beach full of people with bathing suits?" Jim said, looking back.

"No, the next beach is several miles away. This beautiful place is all ours, at least for now. You want to walk down into the surf?"

Jim followed Jane as they walked hip-deep into the water.

"It feels different with the waves lapping directly against my balls," Jim said. "It's kind of nice."

"It feels awful good on my pussy too. In fact, the rhythmic wave action is so erotic I'm starting to get horny."

Jane turned towards Jim and put her arms around Jim's neck to give him a deep, passionate kiss. Her hard nipples dug into his chest, causing his dick to harden. The deeper she kissed him, the more eagerly his cock pressed against her thighs in search of her squirming pussy.

Jane broke off the kiss, grabbed his dick, and pulled him further into the surf.

When they got out to where the water was chest-high, she turned and kissed him again. Putting one arm around his neck, she used her free hand to massage his dick to full salute. It did not take long. Jane's tits bounced up and down thanks to the waves, forcing her hard nipples to slide repeatedly across Jim's chest.

"No one is close enough to us to determine what we're doing." Her breath was hot in his ear.

"I've always dreamed of fucking in the ocean." She then raised her buoyant body and wrapped her legs around his hips, and his dick thrust eagerly into her waiting cunt.

She then skootched herself up and down on his dick, causing him to fuck in and out of her cunt, in a standing position. For his part, Jim just held on for dear life, spreading his legs enough to keep from being knocked over by the waves. His cock was planted deep into her throbbing slot as she locked her arms around his neck. They kissed so passionately they could feel each other's tongues at the back of their throats.

A beautiful ocean, a beautiful beach, and an even more beautiful girl with her legs wrapped around her man. As her soft tits pressed hard nipples into his chest, she gave him the kind of passionate kisses that curl your toes in the wet sand. Then finally, there was a long slot of a velvety soft pussy, gliding up and down a stiff cock...Heaven!

Before long, they both slammed into thundering climaxes. As the spasms slowed, Jane continued to clutch onto Jim tight. The waist-high surf kept anybody from seeing what they were doing, so there was no need to hurry. She took her time pulling herself off his deflating dick, neither ready for the fuck to end.

Finally, they walked back to the beach. "That was awesome," Jim said.

At the surf's edge, Jane ran her fingers between her thighs. "Wow! No cleanup is necessary; the surf has done it for me."

"This beach is a definite do-over for next weekend," Jane said.

"Fuck, yeah," Jim replied.

It was a long drive home. On the way, Jane said she wanted to stop at an adult video store. A strange request for a female, Jim thought. But why should a guy question the motives of a girl who wanted to go to a XXX store? It couldn't be a bad thing.

When they got inside, she went straight to the adult toy section. After she looked at several different vibrators and dildos, she finally found vibrating panties. It consisted of crotchless women's panties with a small vibrator strapped right over the woman's clit.

"This is what I'm looking for." She smiled.

Jane ordered Jim to strip and shave his balls when they got home.

"What the fuck? No razor has ever been anywhere near my balls. What if I cut something?"

"I shave my pussy all the time and don't have any problems, but I'll help if you want. Trust me. You're going to like my little plan." She pushed the button on the vibrating panties to ensure the battery was fresh.

Jim wasn't sure what they had to do with the surprise. But what the hell? He trusted Jane was planning something they would both enjoy, so off they went to the bathroom.

"Strip off your clothes while I start a warm bath," Jane said, throwing the vibrating panties on the bed.

They had a Jacuzzi-style tub big enough for two. In the past, the two had a lot of fun in that tub, and Jane filled it with about eight inches of warm water.

"Get in." She spoke.

When he did, she stripped and joined him.

They lathered each other up to wash off the sand and suntan lotion. As Jane cleansed his balls and dick, it gave Jim a slight erection. Of course, Jim paid particular attention to Jane's soft boobs and crotch. As he ran the palm of his hand across her pussy, he let a finger part her pussy lips and pop into her cunt hole.

"Slow down, tiger." She spoke. "We'll get there in due time." She reached for two razors and gave one to him.

"So, how do I do this?" He asked.

"Sit up on the edge of the tub and watch me." Jane sat on the opposite edge of the tub. She spread her knees wide, fully exposing her pussy, causing her puffy pink lips to part slightly. Using body shampoo, she generously lathered up the small landing strip of pubic hair and all around her pussy.

"I must touch myself up like this periodically, and it shouldn't be a problem for you." She shaved in short, slow strokes, rinsing the razor frequently in the tub. After she was baby smooth, Jane sat down in the water to wash her pussy off.

"Now, spread your knees wider." She said and lathered up his pubic hair and rubbed the soapy mix around his dick and balls. Jim's dick was starting to rise again.

"Shave in short strokes, like I did, rinsing in the tub water frequently. I would suggest starting at the top, where it's easiest."

Soon, he was as hairless as she was. Jane rinsed his balls and dick with tub water.

"Now turn around, honey. Get on your hands and knees with your butt facing me. I want to ensure the underside of your balls and that hairy ass is shaved too."

"What the hell?" But it was too late to back out, and he started to assume the position.

"On your knees, baby, spread your knees further apart." She tapped his cheeks, and he scooched into place. Again, she lathered him up.

This time she focused on his ass and the underside of his balls. Her slippery hand ran into his crack, and a gentle finger slid across his ass hole. Damn, that felt good, he thought. She shaved and rinsed him in that very personal spot, then gave him a peck on the cheek. "You're no longer hairy, honey. Now let's towel off and go to bed."

As Jim lay on the bed, Jane stood before him and put on the vibrating panties. It made a faint hum when she turned it on. Jim reached up and ran two fingers along her pussy lips through the open crotch of the panties. She reached into the nearby dresser drawer to pull out a small vibrator and some lubricating gel.

"You're pretty wet already," Jim said as he parted her pussy lips, letting a finger dart into her slippery cunt hole.

"The lube isn't for my pussy." She spoke. "I told you I have plans," she said as she inserted the vibrator into her mouth and sucked on it like a kid with a lollipop. She then lowered it to her pussy, pushing his hand away. She turned the vibrator on and inserted it high into her waiting cunt.

"Ahh..." She could not help moaning. Her hips bucked and rolled as she thrust the small vibrator in and out of her cunt. Meanwhile, the clit buzzer on her panties continued to hum. With her free hand, she pushed him backward on the bed. At the same time, she plunged the vibrator all the way inside her cunt, and her sticky pussy lips closed tightly around it.

"Move your butt further towards the middle of the bed." She said as she was already crawling up between his knees.

Jim's dick was rock hard just from watching the show. He did not know what was coming, but I knew it would be good.

Jane grabbed his rigid cock and began to lick the underside. While holding onto his crankshaft, she turned her attention to his now hairless balls as she began to suck them one at a time into her hot mouth.

She stopped for a second. "I've been thinking about this since I saw the guy with the shaved balls on the beach, and I kept thinking about sucking your balls with no hair in the way." She stuck out her tongue and then flicked it along the underside of his twitching dick. Jim moaned in delight.

"Raise your feet in the air and arch your back so your butt sticks up."

"Wow, you have been thinking about this," Jim said.

After he obeyed, she licked the delicate underside of his balls between his sac and asshole. Her hand kept its controlling grip on his dick. Her tongue swept up and down the crack of his ass and across the ass hole. When she let go of his dick, it was so she could spread his ass cheeks wide to let her tongue probe his asshole. Her tongue circled the rim again and again. When she had his tight hole wet with spit, her tongue tip forced its way in, darting in and out several times, a unique erotic sensation that he had never had before.

Jane sat up. "Hold that position."

It was now time to find out what the lube was for. Jane squirted a small amount onto her finger, then greased up the area around his asshole, letting her finger slip in and out several times. This caused Jim to wiggle his butt.

"Hold still, honey." With a giggle, she popped the small vibrator out of her pussy and stuck it high and hard up his ass.

Jim groaned. It had looked so small, but his asshole suddenly felt full. The massaging action of the vibrator wiggling back and forth against his prostate caused his already rock-hard dick to get even more erect. Jane pushed his legs flat on the bed with the little vibrator still wedged and vibrating deep inside his ass. She gripped his throbbing dick, and her tongue returned to the heavily veined underside. By this point, being licked was more of a torture than delight.

"Please!" Jim begged, but she kept licking for what seemed like an eternity. "Dear God, please, oh, fuck! Let me come!"

Smiling a tiny smile, she finally placed her mouth over his crown. She then lurched downward and deep-swallowed the entirety of his throbbing shaft in a single motion. She was sucking so hard that he could see the suction pulling in her cheeks.

Jim ran his hands through Jane's hair as her head bobbed up and down on his shaft. As he watched his dick disappear in and out of her mouth, he felt like he would explode any minute. Jane seemed to sense the tension, and without warning, she would abruptly stop sucking on his dick. Then Jane went back to licking the underside with light flicks of her tongue. Dear God, was she trying to drive him mad? He thought to himself.

Once he was further from the brink, she engulfed his dick a second time. When the build-up got too close, she stopped short of him coming again. His entire body was a pulsating nerve by this point. He wanted to get off so bad, yet he could not quite make it.

She engulfed his dick a third time. This time, her body tensed as the vibrating panties brought her to a climax. She did not stop sucking this time, even though he could feel his climax approaching. But Jane was too busy coming to remember to prevent Jim from coming.

"It's here. I'm coming." He moaned as his dick erupted in an enormous spasm that seemed to pass through his body in several waves. He was shooting a truly volcanic load of cum at the back of her throat. In all her loving greatness, Jane did not stop sucking as he spewed and spewed, and she swallowed and swallowed. It was crazy, the best kind of crazy. On and on, she drank down his salty cum, working her throat hard to suck him dry.

She finished by playfully licking the last drop of cum off the tip of his dick. Then she licked her lips clean like a kid who had been eating an ice cream cone.

"Fuck me. That was the greatest blowjob in the history of the world!" He pulled her over for a hug and a big kiss. He could taste the lingering remains of his salty cum on her lips.

Later that night, they would fuck again and, in the morning, too.

Sunday, they had chores around the house, and Jim had a golf outing scheduled with some of the guys at work. Jane planned to visit her parents. Fuckem, they both thought and put them off so they could go back to the beach a second time.

Sunday's beach outing was just as enjoyable as Saturday's, complete with a long walk along the beach and a fuck in the ocean. Jane really liked the no-clean-up part.

They both decided they wanted to make going to the nude beach a regular weekend event.

Chapter 3

Not as Boring as You Think

It was hard for both of them to concentrate on their work on Monday as they remembered their fabulous time at the beach.

Mike came by Jim's desk to ask how his weekend went. "You missed a great day for golfing, Jim. Sorry, you had to spend it with the old wife doing boring errands."

"Fuck you, Mike. My wife is younger than you, old man. Anyway, I enjoyed spending time with her. I'll be going over to her parents next weekend, so I won't be able to go golfing then either."

"You sound like you're pretty whipped, Jim. The next thing you know, your wife will cut out your fishing. You'll be lucky if you're allowed to watch the game on TV."

Then Betty chimed in, a problem with open-plan offices; everybody has an opinion. "I don't see a problem with a guy who spends a little time with his wife, Betty said. "All Bob did this weekend was golf and watch football. Bob's lucky I didn't run off with the landscaper."

Jim would have loved to be able to tell them the truth about his weekend. It would be worth the fuss just to see the looks on their faces. Especially, Mike, he would shit bricks if he knew Jim had gone to a nude beach. Not once but twice, fucked in the ocean like a couple of dolphins and came home to the raunchiest sex this side of a professional porno video. His weekend was anything but boring, but he knew Jane would not want their private business to become office gossip. So, all he did was excuse himself from getting together with them next weekend.

That evening, Debbie dropped by.

"Where have you two been? I called a couple of times, but you did not answer. I was bored stiff. All John wanted to do all weekend long was to sit at home and watch football on TV. I was going to ask if you wanted to get out and go shopping or something, especially since I thought Jim had golf."

They could confide in Debbie, so Jane told her about her weekend at the nude beach. Jane even showed her the black panties with the built-in vibrator. "The sex has never been better." She spoke.

"Fuck, I'm so jealous of you two. First, you go to a topless beach, and now you go to a nude beach, and the nude beach was all my idea. But do you think I can talk that stick-in-the-mud man of mine into trying anything fun? And I cannot believe the wild sex you two are having! You're having sex more in one weekend than John and me in a year."

Debbie grabbed both of Jane's hands to pull her in closer. "Tell me everything. I want more than what I read on the Internet."

They told her about the nude surfers, the long walk along the surf's edge, the unspoiled beauty, and the endless stretch of beach to the north where the crowds petered out. They even told Debbie about them fucking in the ocean.

"If only John weren't such a bore," Debbie said. "I'd love to check it out, but I guess I'll have to live through your experiences."

As soon as she left the house, Jane turned to Jim. "Perhaps we could take her with us next weekend. We might have to keep our clothes on, and we would definitely not be able to have sex, but I think it would mean a lot to her. She really feels like she's missing out in life."

"You two girls could go without me. Call me a horndog, but I don't necessarily want to visit a nude beach if I have to keep my clothes on and then be left with blue balls."

"No, honey, I wouldn't want to go without you. Besides, the guys might hit on us if they see two women by themselves." Jane squeezed his upper thigh. Jane has a way of making a man see her point of view.

But Jim thought of another complication. "It wouldn't bother you for me to see her naked?"

"Is it that different from you being around the other nude women at the beach? It is not as if you have sex with any of them; all you do is see them the way nature intended. I'm starting to think our society has too much of an issue about naked bodies."

Jane got up and fetched two bottles of beer. They clinked them together, and then she turned a little more serious. "Debbie is my closest friend; she has been down a lot lately, and I think she needs something to cheer her up. That husband of hers acts as if they are already dead. If she decides to take her clothes off to get the full experience, I am okay with it. You can go nude as well. I trust you both, and I know I'll be naked."

"What about John? I know he's a jerk, but wouldn't it be like she was cheating on him?"

"Looking isn't cheating, hon. You and the guys went to that strip club a couple of years ago for Joe's bachelor party, and I don't think you or John considered it cheating."

"You're right. Give Debbie a call."

Of course, Debbie said yes. The plan was pretty straightforward. She told John that she and Jane would spend Saturday afternoon at the beach together. She just didn't mention it was a nude beach, much less that Jim tagged along. Jane picked up Debbie at her place while Jim packed the cooler. It might have seemed sneaky, but they did not want to arouse John's suspicions. Debbie wore an older two-piece bikini out of the house. It was a little chillier than the previous weekend, but it was bright and sunny, and the nude beach's parking lot was packed again. Jim had to drop off the ladies and then take the car back to the previous lot, just as if they were regulars.

You could hear the doubt in Debbie's voice as Jim drove off. "Everybody looks fully clothed to me, Jane."

"Trust me, Debbie," Jane said. "On the other side of the dune crossover, it's a different world."

After Jim hiked back, they gathered their stuff to head for the crossover. Or should you say Jim gathered up their stuff? Jane was in the lead, followed by Debbie, and Jim was the pack mule bringing up the rear.

As soon as they reached the top of the crossover, Debbie's gaze swung to the left to stare at all the beachgoers walking about and sunbathing au naturel.

"Well, Debbie, here we are," Jane said. "You can still back out, and we can visit one of the other beaches we passed, back away."

"No way am I backing out now."

"Then follow me. Let us look for a place that is not too crowded. When we were here last weekend, the further you got away from the crossover, the fewer the people until you got to the gay cruising spot. Almost no one went on further than that. So, if you're looking for more privacy..."

"Sounds like a plan, Jane," Debbie said. "Let's go."

Easy for them to say, Jim thought. The girls were not the pack mule lugging all their stuff through the sand to the end of the beach. Finally, they got to a quiet spot where he could put their stuff down.

They spread their blankets in a row with Jane's in the middle and all applied sunscreens. Then, the three of them sat silently, looking out at the ocean. They had not planned the disrobing part and did not expect it to be so awkward.

"You girls need some water?" Jim handed around chilled bottles from the cooler.

While they drank, the silence continued as they looked out at the water. No one was sure what the others were thinking, but sure as shit, no one was thinking about the ocean.

Jim, for one, was thinking like a man and how Debbie had a great body with big boobs. What would she look like nude? Did her plump titties boast large nipples? Are her aureoles darker than Jane's? Was her crotch neatly trimmed or fully shaved? Would she ever get around to taking her top off? Or even possibly her bottoms off, so he could find out?

Jane crumpled up her empty water bottle and dropped it on the beach blanket. "I don't know about the rest of you clowns, but I came here to get an all-over tan." She untied her top and let it fall. Then she wiggled out of her bottoms.

"Are you sure it's all right for me to take off my top in front of Jim?"

"He's a big boy," Jane said. "I assume he knows why we're here. I am okay with it if he is okay with it. Are you okay with it, honey?"

Great, Jim thought to himself. It's one of those loaded questions women like to ask guys.

"Sure." He thought a simple, short answer was the best and then sprawled out on his back. Closing his eyes, he tried to pretend he just wanted to sunbathe and did not give a shit either way about whether or not Debbie got naked.

"I'm not ready to take my bottoms off," Debbie admitted. "But I don't want to look like a total gawker, so..." she said as her voice trailed off.

After a moment or two, Jim took a sneak peek, and her top was indeed gone. Unfortunately, all he could see from where he was sitting was her bareback and the side of one of her enormous boobs. She was sitting, leaning forward with her folded arms resting on her knees. The hunched position hid her more effectively than the skimpy bikini top. From time to time, she sipped nervously at her water, not as if she was thirsty but more as if she just wanted an excuse to sit that way.

Even though they were in broad daylight, on a wide-open beach, Jim felt like he was some sort of peeping Tom as he tried to get glimpses of Debbie and the other nude people walking about. Her shyness was definitely making things uncomfortable. Finally, Debbie turned towards Jane, allowing Jim to get a quick look at her enormous jugs. They were everything he had imagined, bountiful and unsaggable, with large dark aureoles topped with long nipples.

"I think I'm ready to take a stroll along the beach." She spoke.

Jane stood up and struck a pose. She liked being the bold one as it made her feel a little more sophisticated. "All right, but I'm not going to be the only one fully nude. You two need to join me, or I will have to put my bikini back on."

Jim looked over at Debbie, and she looked at Jim. She was still trying to cover her boobs with her arms without looking too obvious. Both waited for the other to make the first move.

It was not happening as Jim and Debbie both looked at Jane.

"Oh, for fuck's sake," Jane said. "Enough. You would think the two of you were a couple of little kids who had never seen a naked body before. Grow the fuck up. Now, I want both of you to stand up." She motioned with her hands. "Come on. Up, up, up!"

They stood about an arm's length away from each other. Debbie continued to hold her right arm across her boobs, trying to cover them up, a hopeless task due to their enormous size.

"Now turn around with your backs to each other and look straight ahead. Oh, and Debbie, put your fucking arms down! Most women would want to show off what you've got."

They obeyed, although Debbie did not lower her arm until she was facing away.

"Jeez, Jim, those big fucking trunks have got to go." Jane grabbed his trunks at the waistband and yanked them down over his ass.

"You have a cute, tight ass. It's all mine, and I intend to show it off. The equipment in front isn't half bad either."

He was not sure if that last comment was a compliment or not. Either way, his trunks were down at his ankles.

"Raise your right foot." Jane pulled the trunks free from his foot.

"Now lift your left foot. No peeking, Debbie. Both of you keep looking straight ahead." Jane pulled the trunks away. Jim stood there, totally naked and a bit nervous.

Sure, he was naked last week, but the people around him were total strangers, and he would never see any of them again. But Debbie was a female friend of his wife, whom he knew he would have to face many times in the future.

"Here, you hold on to these," Jane said, handing Debbie Jim's trunks. "I'm going to remove your bottoms, too. You have a gorgeous body, and you should show it off. From what you have told me, John does not look at your naked body much, and you might as well let the rest of the world enjoy it a little."

"I don't know, Jane..." Debbie sounded like she was getting cold feet.

Jim was starting to regret that they had invited her.

"What don't you know?" Jane said. "You rode over an hour to get here, so you must be somewhat curious. So just let loose and let yourself enjoy the fresh air." Jane did not wait for an answer, and Jim could hear Debbie's bikini bottoms sliding down. Jane gave her the same commands to lift her feet one at a time, then handed him Debbie's bikini bottom.

"There, you both have each other's bottoms in your hands. Hold them down at your sides, not in front of you, so that I can see those hot bodies. Good. Good!" Jane had the makings of a halfway decent dominatrix as she quickly fell into the habit of giving the orders.

Jane picked up a towel and held it between Jim and Debbie. "Both of you turn and face the ocean."

Jim and Debbie did as she directed, but both strained to peek at the other. However, they could only see Jane from the corner of their eyes. She was holding her beach towel as if she was a matador, a nude female matador.

"I can see that both of you are trying to peek. Therefore, you know I am holding my towel to block your view of each other. Now turn and face the towel."

They obeyed. Due to the large towel blocking the view, all Jim and Debbie could see of each other were their feet and head. "Keep your hands at your sides." Jane tried to look stern. "Ole."

She flung the towel away, revealing to Debbie Jim's slender physique with his tight, firm butt, and Jim finally was given a full-frontal view of all Debbie's stunning beauty, with her massive pendulous boobs to go with a mound waxed as smooth as a baby's ass.

"Now, children, I want each of you to look at each other. Now let's take a good look at the various body parts, paying close attention to those different from your own." Jane said as her voice turned teacherish like a First-grade teacher.

However, Jane was welcome to talk down to them as if they were children all she wanted, as long as Jim got to drool over Debbie's body. This little game she was playing gave them an excellent opportunity to stare at each other's bodies. "As you can see, Debbie, Jimmy is a boy, and boys have penises. This is his penis." Jane pointed to Jim's, which responded with a happy twitch of excitement.

"It's also sometimes referred to as a dick, cock, prick, pecker, peter, tool, shaft, and many others. Behind his penis are his testicles, two of them in a soft sack. Frequently, they are called balls or nuts. In my case, I refer to them as the family jewels. Please do not touch them, as they are mine, all mine. Now Jimmy, turn around so she can see your cute little ass. Nice and tight, isn't it, Debbie?" Jane patted his left cheek. "Now, turn back around, Jimmy."

Now, it was Jim's turn for a lesson. "Jimmy, Debbie is a girl. Girls here have two breasts, sometimes called bosom, tits, titties, boobs, or knockers. Give them a gentle shake, Debbie, so Jimmy can see how they move." Debbie gave her boobs a light shake. Because of their size, they wobbled for several seconds. Dear God, Jim just wanted to reach out and squeeze them. Jim assumed John must be gay, impotent, dead, or fucking crazy if he would rather watch TV than screw his drop-dead gorgeous wife every minute of the day!

"Down here, Jimmy is a girl's vagina. Spread your feet a little further apart, Debbie, so that Jimmy can get a better view." Debbie planted her feet about fourteen inches apart, and her toes dug into the sand. As a result, he could clearly see how her pussy lips protruded slightly below her love mound. "This is a girl's vagina. It, too, has multiple names, such as pussy, cunt, slit, twat, box, and many more. Now turn around and wiggle your ass."

As instructed, she gave Jim an iconic rear view of feminine beauty. Her ass had just the right wobble as she turned. Talk about an ass to die for.

"You won't have to worry about getting that hot naked butt of yours in trouble while you're here, Debbie. I'm sure Jimmy will be keeping a close eye on it."

She got that right.

"Know, let's stroll along the water's edge," Jane said. "I don't want to get too wet with this breeze, so I'm not going in very deep. But it's still a gorgeous day for a walk."

They walked north, away from the larger group of people near the parking lot. After about an hour, Jane stopped cold. "I think I drank too much water."

Debbie looked unsettled. "I've got to go too."

The one thing about a lovely undeveloped beach is that you do not have a lot of convenient toilets.

The ladies looked around. "Shit, Debbie, it's ninety minutes back the way we came to the nearest public restroom. And it is even further if we keep going north," Jane said as she recalled the details of the maps.

"Looks like you girls got a problem," Jim said. "I guess you'll just have to go behind one of those bushes over there."

"You perv, those bushes are only knee-high." Jane took Debbie's arm. "We'll just go on the other side of the dune."

Jim noted the posted signs to stay off the dune to protect it from erosion, but he knew better than to say anything.

When they got high enough to look over the dune, Jane stopped. "Oh shit." She said, and they both turned around and scrambled back.

"What's the matter?" Jim asked. "Is the park ranger giving tickets?"

"No, but it's just as bad. There is a lagoon on the other side, with not one but two boats full of fishermen, and they'll spot us for sure."

Debbie shrugged. There was only one logical solution. "We'll just have to wade out waist-deep into the water to do our business, as I don't have a better idea."

They were not even knee-deep as they splashed into the water before they started shrieking.

"Shit, this water is cold," Jane said. She scrambled back toward shore again.

Debbie was right behind her. They were shivering violently and bouncing up and down like little girls, but there was nothing little about their stiff nipples.

"Fuck it," Jane said. "I'm just going to pee right here." Jane spread her legs about two feet apart in ankle-deep cold water and stood motionless for several seconds. Apparently, she was having trouble going in front of an audience. Although Jim and Jane were married, they did not make a point of watching each other piss.

She finally closed her eyes to focus. A trickle of golden pee started to dribble out, and soon, it became a forceful stream that splashed into the water to make a patch of frothy foam.

"Ahh, much better," Jane said as she splashed a hand full of water onto her pussy to rinse off. In the process, she spread her knees, giving the most delightful view.

"Great, Jane. What the fuck am I supposed to do?" Debbie squirmed and held her crotch as she looked directly at Jim.

"Don't let my horny husband slow you down," Jane said. "Do whatever you have to do. We are all three naked as jaybirds here, anyway. As you can see, I wasn't going to go very far into that cold water and get all wet on this windy day!"

Debbie stepped ankle-deep into the water and spread her legs. She did not bother to turn her back or ask Jim to look away. Interestingly, it was as if she was deliberately putting on a show for him to watch. The only problem is nothing happened.

"I've got to go, but I can't relax." She licked a finger and tried massaging her pee hole with her wet digit. Finally, the pee began to flow, but it did not go straight into the water. And instead, it sprayed down her inner thigh.

"Oh shit." She spread her knees further apart. At last, she was peeing straight down in a steady stream. "I got pee all over my leg."

"Just splash some water on it to rinse off," Jane said. "You'll dry off soon."

The three spent the rest of the afternoon enjoying the beach in complete clothes-free freedom. The three might have been loose enough to pee in front of each other, but Jane and Jim did not fuck in the ocean like last time. Instead, they enjoyed being nude in each other's company, stealing glances at each other's bodies and the others at the beach. Jim found Debbie's curves particularly fun to watch. Her ass knew how to bounce and sway as seductively as her boobs.

Afterward, they went to Jim and Jane's house to drop Jim off. Then Jane went with Debbie to drop off Debbie at her house, keeping her bathing suit on so as not to tip John off that they had gone home to drop Jim off first. After all, as far as John knew, Jim was never at the beach with them.

When Jane returned home, Jim was waiting in the living room, still wearing nothing but his swim trunks. His wife planted a big, wet kiss on his mouth while grabbing him by the crotch.

"I'm glad you're nothing like Debbie's husband. He did not even know she was gone all afternoon. He was completely wrapped up in a football game on the tube, and I bet you have been fantasizing about fucking Debbie all day long, haven't you, baby? You're a naughty, naughty little boy." As she massaged his cock through the fabric, Jim was getting stiffer and stiffer. Jane dropped to her knees, yanked down his trunks using both hands and aimed his prick at her wanton mouth.

Jim kicked the trunks away from his ankles and spread his feet slightly. As he got more worked up, he clutched the back of her head to encourage her face to slide further down his cock.

"Fuck." Jim groaned as he tilted his head back and sighed contently.

Jim decided the fucking bikini top had to go, and he tugged it away as she continued to suck. She took the hint and used her free hand to help wiggle her bikini bottom off her butt. Once it was past her knees, she kicked it away without taking his cock out of her mouth.

She then pushed him back onto the couch, where he sat with his butt on the edge of the bed, giving her full access to his balls and cock. She would deepthroat his prick and then pull it out of her mouth to tease the tip. Meanwhile, she kept one hand busy massaging his balls.

Jane wanted off, too, so she spat his dick out of her mouth before he exploded. Jim whimpered as she scrambled forward to place one knee on each side of his hip. Grabbing his dick again, Jane guided it to her sopping wet cunt to impale herself hard. Jane began to ride him, balancing herself with one hand on the back of the coach and the other squeezing her right breast. Each time she bounced up, she rose almost all the way off his dick, leaving only the tip in her pussy. She leaned forward and pressed a boob into Jim's waiting mouth each time.

"I know. You have fantasized about sucking on Debbie's big boobs all day, and it was obvious from the guilty way you stole quick glances at them."

Jim could not deny it if he wanted to, as his mouth was full of his wife's perfectly edible left boob. He rolled the flat of his tongue around the hard nipple as he sucked on her tasty flesh. However, he was not entirely gagged as a soft moan of pleasure managed to escape from the back of his throat.

Jane sat down hard on Jim's dick and began to fuck, bouncing rhythmically up and down. He placed his hands on her soft ass as it rose and fell, up and down, on his throbbing boner. Thanks to his wife's nasty suggestion, Jim could not stop imagining that it was Debbie on top of him. He could not stop picturing his dick thrusting in and out of Debbie's pussy. Jane tensed. Her pussy gripped his dick tightly as she began to climax. She lost the rhythm for a while and then found it again. Up and down, forward and back.

Jim's whole body felt like a hard-on, and he could not hold back anymore as he released what felt like a gallon of cum into Jane's eager pussy. As Jim shuddered to a stop, Jane rolled off him. Both were exhausted. Jane snuggled by his side, too tired to jump up instantly to clean up the mess. Today she was content to let their fuck juices drool out of her full pussy and all over the couch.

"That was fun," Jane said.

Over the next several weeks, Jane and Jim became regulars at the nude beach. Most guys at work thought Jim was getting pretty pussy-whipped since he had stopped golfing and fishing.

Rachel and some other women thought it was nice that he spent more time with his wife. However, they questioned why they had not run into them at the malls and movies, which Jim often used as an excuse for not hanging out with the guys.

Chapter 4
New Adventure

They became more comfortable as they got more into the clothes-free lifestyle. Soon, Jim and Jane tried a couple of other nude beaches on the Florida coast. All further away than the first beach we went to. And Debbie always wanted the latest updates on our adventures. Debbie asked to go when they said they would try Haulover Beach down by Miami. It was the largest nude beach in Florida. Of course, Jane said yes. Jane knew Jim would want another opportunity to see Debbie's gorgeous ass and boobs just as much as Debbie wanted to go.

Haulover is a large beach, but full nudity was only allowed in a small clothing-optional area at the north end. As a result, the nude area was super crowded. But the three of us found a small clearing, put up our umbrella, and got comfortable. It definitely was not as relaxing as the other beaches, with uncrowded and leisurely strolls along the surf. But it was much more enjoyable for people watching.

Soon after we got comfortable, two young white couples in their twenties, with a lot of beach gear, strolled by and set up in front of us. All four were heavily tanned. But when they removed their suits, it was apparent the couple that walked in front were regulars, having all-over tans. The other couple was clearly more hesitant to remove their suits, and when they removed the bottoms, they had alabaster white butts, definitely first-timers. We were already learning nudist jargon, and these nubies were sometimes called cotton tails.

The two women set up beach loungers, and for the rest of the day, all we saw of them were the back of their heads. The two guys set up a cornhole game and began to play. Not that I check out other men, but they were clearly well-toned examples of the muscular male Physique. Soon, a black female security woman in her mid-fifties driving a beach buggy with security makings drove by. She stopped and turned around, and asked to check their cooler. At first, we were not sure what she was looking for, especially since she hadn't asked to check our cooler. The guys then gave her a half-hour instruction about the finer points of playing cornhole. A half-hour for cornhole instructions! Obviously, it wasn't the cooler or the game she was interested in.

Soon, another people-watching event took place. What looked to be five college-age girls showed up to our right with beach chairs. Unlike the rest of the beachgoers in the nude-allowed area, they did not immediately strip out of their suits. As it is a clothing-optional beach, that was their option. Obviously, they were not interested in going nude themselves and wanted to check out a nude beach without participating. Soon, they were surrounded by several similar-age guys who encouraged them to go naked. Initially, they resisted, but then one of the guys encouraged them to at least go topless. Soon, one girl eventually took off her top, and soon the others followed, egged on by the first girl's encouragement. The girls then went down by the water's edge and splashed through the surf. When they returned to their beach chairs, they were immediately encouraged by the guys to take their bottoms off. The same girl who took the lead in removing her top also took the lead in taking off her bottoms, and the other four followed. They then went back down to the water's edge to splash about again. But they didn't stop there. Soon, all five were using cell phones to have their photos taken in Playboy-style poses. Debbie, Jane, and I wondered what their mothers would say if, or more likely when, they saw the photos.

Although the people-watching at Haulover was fun and interesting, it wasn't the relaxing experience with the post-sexual release we had come to enjoy as nudists.

Although Jim and Jane still enjoyed the occasional sex in the surf, the long drive tended to be tiring. As the novelty wore off, they found themselves pretty exhausted by the time they got home, especially Haulover Beach, which was over two hours away. As a result, they were not as interested in sex as they were when first starting to go to the nude beaches.

One evening after their latest trip to the beach, Jane brought up a conversation she had had with Debbie earlier. "Jim, I was talking to Debbie, feeling she was someone we could confide in regarding our new-found adventures. I told her that because of the long drive home, we were not having passionate sex like when we first started going to the nude beaches. At first, Debbie was glad not to be alone in the no-sex department."

"What do you mean, no ...."

"Before you get your balls all out of round, I set her straight and told her about last night." Jane gave him a quick peck on the cheek as she gently massaged his crotch.

"Good," Jim said. "I'm glad you set her straight. But I'm not sure she needs to know all our business."

"Debbie's my best friend, and I have to talk to somebody. She suggested we try one of those nudist resorts we found on the Internet. The one near Orlando, the Orange Blossom Resort, advertised that it had quite a few amenities, including two pools, restaurants, a private lake, and more. They also have events that include live bands, DJs, and other activities."

"Jane, it's over an hour away, and we'd still have a long drive home, just in another direction."

"It's a full resort, with a hotel for overnight guests. We can spend the night and not have to return until the next day." Her hand made a convincing argument as she massaged his crotch more firmly.

"You sold me. Fine, let's book a room this weekend." Jim said. "But right now, I need to take care of this hard-on you gave me." He picked her up and flung her over his shoulder like a caveman taking a woman back to his cave for a good fucking.

Going to their bedroom, he flung her down on the bed. She sat up as he undid his belt. She grabbed the top of his jeans and shorts and pulled everything down to his knees in one fell swoop. As she did, Jim's rapidly hardening member sprang up, slapping her in the face. Her mouth took the hint. Opening wide, she was engulfing its entire length as he was still stepping out of his shorts and jeans. He pushed her back on the bed and yanked her short skirt over her waist to reveal her wet black lace panties. Jim's nostrils flared from the pungent aroma of a woman with a ready-to-be-fucked pussy. Pushing apart her knees, he pulled the soaked crotch of the panties to the side and guided his rigid dick between her moist pussy lips. He slid deep into her slippery wet pussy in an instant. He began rapidly ramming in and out in long thrusts. Jane wrapped her legs around his back and her arms around his neck. She had to hold on tight because they were already starting to come. Within a few more strokes, He was unloading stream after stream of steaming hot cum into her churning pussy.

Jane took off her panties and used them to wipe her cum-filled pussy clean. Then she stripped out of the rest of her clothes.

"If I'm going to be a real nudist, I might just as well start going nude around the house."

Jane made the reservations for Saturday night. Check-in was at 3:00 pm, and check-out would be on Sunday at noon. It should be plenty of time to investigate the scene.

Come Saturday, they were ready for their new adventure.

"What do you pack when going to a nudist resort?" Jim asked.

"I guess just a toothbrush."

They headed out the door with only a zip-lock bag containing two toothbrushes and a small tube of toothpaste, which Jane stuffed in her purse with her makeup.

An hour later, they were driving down a backcountry road flanked by hedge-like palmettos on both sides. The entrance drive, marked only by a small sign, was hidden in a break between the palmettos, and they almost passed it. It had the name Orange Blossom Resort and a phone number, but there was no indication it was a nudist resort.

Turning into the drive, they saw a guard booth with a small white railway-style crossing gate just beyond it. The guard sitting inside was an older, fully clothed man. A small sticker in the window said it was a clothing-optional nudist resort, the first real clue that they were on the right track.

Jim rolled down the car's window, gave him their names, and told him they had reservations for tonight. He looked it up on his computer and gave them directions to the check-in building about a quarter mile down and on the left. As they proceeded, they could not see anything but palmettos. As the drive wound around more palmettos and some strategically placed bushes that blocked the view from the road, they spotted several nude couples walking about.

Most had towels. Some women wrapped the towels around their waist as if they were wearing a skirt. Others flung them over their shoulders without attempting to cover any of their so-called private parts. Most of the guys were also bare ass with towels over their shoulders. One oddball wore a tee shirt but nothing below. It was as if he got dressed hurriedly and forgot to put his pants on.

"I wonder if any people have ever come here, not realizing it was nude," Jane said. "It would be easy to miss the small sign in the booth window."

"I don't know, Jane, but it would be fun to see their reaction if they ever did."

They felt a little self-conscious, getting out of the car since they were the only people around who were fully clothed. The front desk clerks were also naked, causing them to feel even more out of place. Jim and Jane told them they had been to nude beaches before, but this was their first nudist resort. The elderly female clerk who waited on them asked if they had brought towels. "It's considered proper nudist etiquette to carry a towel to sit or lounge on." She spoke. Now they knew why most of the people outside had towels.

"No," Jane said. "All we brought were two toothbrushes and a small tube of toothpaste."

"We do sell towels." The clerk pointed to the rack behind them.

They selected a couple of towels with the resort's logo, 'Sun Your Buns at The Orange Blossom,' under a sketch of nude sunbathers lying face down to show off bare butts.

The clerk handed them two wristbands with room keys and a barcode tag to wear on their wrist. It was explained that they could use it to charge for food and drink. Since they would not have pockets for money or keys, that seemed like a good idea. She also gave them directions to their room.

"You came on a good night." The clerk said. "We're having a dance party this evening with a live band." That sounded interesting, they thought.

Their room was on the ground floor of the building, just down the drive from the office. It looked like any other hotel room with two full-size beds, a TV, a bath, and a small table.

"They must rent these rooms out to more than a single couple," Jane said, giving Jim a strange look. "It seems a little cozy. Do you think the couples would sleep in the nude?"

"I don't know how much sleep they'd plan on getting."

"You guys all think alike. Let's get out of our clothes and check this place out."

Stripping naked, they put the keys on their wrists. Jane got cold feet for a minute. "Okay, Jim, I guess I'm ready, but would you mind looking to make sure no one is there when we first step out? I need to get used to this."

Peeking out the window, Jim saw an old lady on a bike.

"This is fucking hilarious, Jane. Outside is an old lady riding a bike with a small dog in the basket in the front. She looks just like the old lady on the bike from 'The Wizard of Oz' except she's completely nude."

Jane pulled the curtain further open. "It doesn't look like you'll have to worry about getting an accidental erection here." She spoke. "But if that old lady can ride around nude with her big droopy tits hanging down almost to her knees, then I can do this."

They walked out wearing only the towels over their shoulders and the room keys on their wrists.

First, they went to the Bare Buns Bar & Grill, located next to a large outdoor pool. The bartender simply asked them what they wanted and scanned the barcode they wore around their wrists.

"That was easy," Jane said. "I like not having to carry cash or show I.D., as it would have been a little hard to do in our current state. Let's go over to the pool."

Besides rows of lounge chairs around the large pool, behind the chairs were several small buildings and gazebos. The first building was a recreation room with a pool and ping-pong tables. Next was a retail shop named Bare Necessities Apparel. What kind of apparel does a clothing store sell at a nudist resort? They both had to find out.

The answer was hats, sandals, and not much for in between.

After that, there was a small building with the sign Bare Essence Massage. This building had several large floor-to-ceiling windows. The blinds were pulled entirely back, giving someone watching on the outside a full view inside. The French-style entrance doors also stood wide open. In the center of the room were two massage tables. One table was empty. At the other table, a tall, muscular, shirtless male masseur in tight-fitting jeans was giving a massage to a female customer. She was lying face-up on a massage table, totally nude, except for a small towel spread over her crotch.

A petite but well-endowed topless brunette wearing short shorts waited by the entrance.

"Hello, welcome to Bare Essence Massage; my name is Vicki."

She pointed to the open table. "Can I interest either of you two in a massage? I can take one of you right now."

"Bruce is just finishing up with his customer." Vicki gestured his way. "He can take the other in a minute or two."

Jane was smiling and nodding.

"I guess we're both getting a massage," Jim said.

"I like a firm massage," Jane said. "So, I prefer a male. Why don't you go with Vicki, Jim?"

Jim wondered if she knew how obvious it was that she wanted Bruce's strong hands all over her body. "Fine by me. I'd rather be worked on by a cute brunette any day of the week," Jim said, going to Vicki's table. She immediately covered his butt with a small towel when he lay on the table.

"What's your name, honey?" She asked as she started at his neck. Jim could already tell she was just as capable of a firm massage as anybody else.

"Jim." He replied as he began to engage in small talk. Although the massage was excellent, it was difficult for him to relax, knowing that Vicki's succulent naked boobs were only inches away. When she was ready for the turn, she held the small towel slightly above his rear and asked him to roll over. Now, his crotch was covered.

Jim finally broke down to ask the obvious question. "What's with the towel? This is a nudist resort, and I walked in here butt naked, and it's nothing you haven't already seen."

"It's a Florida state law that a therapist must keep the genitals of the customer covered." She chuckled.

Jim was vaguely aware of his wife on the adjacent table. From time to time, she gasped a little, and Jim gathered she was enjoying her treatment even more than he was enjoying his. Jim, unfortunately, was hampered by having to keep thinking of stock market prices to prevent his semi from becoming a full-on woody. After they left the Bare Essence, they found a couple of lounge chairs by the pool where they could soak up some rays. Observing proper nudist etiquette, they first spread towels out across the chair. With drinks in hand, they began making idle chat about the other guests. Bathing suits were not allowed in the pool, so everyone swimming was nude. Most guests walking by were also totally naked, although some women had towels wrapped around them.

"Jane, let's get a woman's take on this." He said. "Some women walk around with their towels wrapped around their boobs, hanging down low enough to cover their crotch. Some just wrap it around their waist, leaving their boobs uncovered. Still, others drape it over their shoulders, like most of the guys. Why do you think that is?"

"The ones with the towels wrapped around their waists are a bit prudish, but they are enjoying the topless freedom you guys can have any time. The ones with the towels covering everything are just plain prudish. As for me, I am a fling-it-over-the-shoulder kind of gal, as I want to enjoy total clothes-free freedom!"

A hostess wearing nothing but an apron asked them if we would like another round, to which they both said yes.

"Jim, this is the life. I could see myself being here in the buff all the time, and I dread having to put my clothes back on when we must leave."

After dinner, the live band, Bare Assets, started to play in the bar. They were hot... and not just music. It was a five-piece with three sexy women and two good-looking hunks. Most of their music was just as hot. Typically, neither cared much for country music, but the song 'Save a Horse - Ride a Cowboy' has a lot more impact when sung by a hot babe wearing only a cowboy hat and boots. They also played a lot of classic rock as well as a lot of new stuff.

Furthermore, it did not hurt that the dance floor was crowded with naked couples dancing to the music. They ordered drinks and sat down to watch. Quite a few others were doing the same. At first, there were definitely more watchers than dancers, but there was still plenty to look at. Both guys and girls were out on the dance floor, shaking their stuff. Jane was openly studying the guy's butts and crotches. Jim obviously kept a closer eye on the women, not knowing whether to watch shaking butts or jiggling boobs.

On the third song, a new couple entered the dance floor.

"Hey, look, Jane. It's Vicki and Bruce from the Bare Essence Massage." Now, she did not have on her short shorts, and Bruce did not have on his tight-fitting jeans.

"Oh, I see his package matches the rest of his body—big." Jane smiled.

Several more couples entered the dance floor when a slow dance came up. Like most guys, Jim was not as eager to get out on the dance floor as the girls were. However, it did not take him long to see that dancing with your bare-chested babe was a hot thing.

"Want to dance, honey?" He asked Jane, who readily accepted the offer. Now, the dance floor was getting crowded.

Slow dancing with Jane's bare tits against his chest was a definite turn-on. Jane's nipples got harder and harder. When Jim sneakily looked around, he could see the other women's nipples getting just as stiff. His mind flashed back to school dances when he would slow dance with a girl and wonder if that was her nipple he could feel through her top. Here, there was no question. Jane's nipple kept rubbing more and more assertively into his chest. Bruce and some other guys were also taking some liberties with their hands, slipping them down to their partners' bare butt cheeks. This seemed like a good idea—at least at first. Again, Jim's mind flashed back to school, where the guys would try to hold on to the girl's butt, but hot damn, this ass was bare.

This was starting to be too much of a turn-on for Jim, as his dick was getting stiff. He was so stiff he had to back off.

"Come back here, you," Jane said. She playfully grabbed his hand and put it back on her shapely ass. However, she understood when he whispered into her ear. "I already have a bit of a booner baby, and don't make it worse."

Jim also got turned on when he occasionally bumped butts with one of the female dancers. He did not think he bumped into any guys, as the guys were more concerned about keeping their distance from each other. The girls did not seem to care, some of whom appeared to go out of their way to rub butts with others.

They danced for several hours, with Jim's dick being semi-hard most of the evening. Finally, Jane took mercy on him. "I think we should go back to our room."

He knew, by the way, she said that she did not intend to go to sleep.

They hurried back. Since both were already naked, this would not take long. As soon as the door was closed, Jane pulled Jim down on the bed.

"Get over here and fuck me," Jane said as she fell backward. Jim wasted no time doing as told. Jim came down on top of her, landing one knee between her thighs and his hands on her shoulders. Their faces went into an immediate lip-lock with tongues intertwining.

Jim reached down to her crotch to run his fingers through her pussy.

"Fuck, you are so wet."

"That's why I had to come back. I feared some of my cunt juices would start running down my thigh." She wrapped her arms around his back and gave him another passionate kiss.

Gasping for breath, Jim started to slide down her body. First, he made several brief love pecks on her neck before proceeding to her boobs. Jim took turns kissing each of her nipples and then wet-kissed his way to her belly. As he approached her love mound, he gently pushed her thighs apart and nibbled from the top of her landing strip to her protruding clit. He circled his tongue around the hard-little knob before continuing down to the wet gash of her pussy.

"Oh, yes, Jim… Eat me… Eat me!" Jane was screaming. Jim hoped this hotel had good soundproofing, as Jane was so excited, she was screaming sounds of sexual passion.

As she got even hotter, she ran both hands down over her belly to her clit. Her fingertips pushed her love button while his tongue slithered up and down her gash. She held the lips of her pussy apart to urge him on. In a sudden, spontaneous moment, probably prompted by a depraved sexual fantasy, she grabbed onto his head with both her hands and crushed his face into her cunt. Wrapping her legs around his neck, she arched her back and humped herself on his driving tongue. The vibrations working through her thighs made it clear that she was building to a powerful orgasm.

An intense feminine scent from Jane's oozing slit was flooding the room. It was driving Jim mad as he devoured her pussy. His tongue stroked up and down between her cunt lips, lapped up her sex from asshole to clit. He stopped long enough to ram his oral digit inside her trembling core. Each time Jim did that, Jane would clench her pussy muscles hard enough to grip the tip of Jim's tongue. That encouraged Jim to keep tongue fucking her that way. Still, he could not occasionally resist slipping his tongue out to flutter against her clit. Jane started coming again as he pressed hard against the swollen pink bud.

When she was finally finished screaming in ecstasy, he lifted his face from her crotch and untangled himself from her gripping thighs. A combination of spit and pussy cream leaked out of her pussy. A river of sex juice ran down her ass cheeks, soaking the bedspread.

Standing up, Jim guided his dick into her gaping pussy, easily sliding in balls-deep on the first thrust. She had never been more open. He thrust in and out so smoothly that his balls slapped audibly against her juice-covered ass. Her soft, slippery inner walls were warm and inviting as they gripped his dick.

"I'm getting close," Jim said. "Oh God, I'm getting close!" He had been holding back all evening and could not hold back any longer.

With a groan, he allowed himself to slam over the edge and empty deep inside her hot wet pussy in several intense spasms.

Jane hugged him tightly. Her mouth clamped over his to give him a long, passionate kiss as he slumped. They could both feel his slowly deflating dick slip from her pussy.

Jim finally rolled off her exhausted, ready to sleep for a year.

Jim closed his eyes. Then, off, in the distance, he could hear soft music as the band started up again.

"Jane, do you want to go back out to dance?"

"Hell yeah! And the cool thing about it is we don't even have to get dressed. Although we might have to come back to our room for a quick fuck, every once in a while."

She stood up, and cum poured down her leg as she hurried for a warm wet cloth to wipe herself clean.

"Jim, honey, I think we've found our new weekend retreat. I can't wait to tell Debbie all about this place."

Thank you for reading!

W.E. Sinful - Please review

If you have suggestions or comments, feel free to email us at D2@DJRV.com.

Other books by W.E. Sinful

Debbie Wants to Go - The second book of the Orange Blossom series. After their first trip to the Orange Blossom nudist resort, Jim and Jane tell Debbie about it. She is completely taken by their description of the band that played in the nude. Jane then asked if she wanted to join them on their next trip to the Orange Blossom. Debbie eagerly agrees and does the Orange Blossom in a big way as she releases her pent-up sexual desires.

The Bare Assets Band -The third book of the Orange Blossom series. Readers are introduced to the band that plays in the nude. They started as a regular nightclub five-piece. Still, they had to overcome their modesty when the financial need required them to accept an offer to play at the Orange Blossom Nudist Resort. They end up doing much more than just becoming nudists...

What Did You Do This Weekend? – In the fourth book of the series, Rachel, a co-worker of Jim's, finds out that Jim and his wife Jane have a naked secret, that of being nudists. After overcoming their initial embarrassment of being discovered, Jim and Jane invite Rachel and her husband to the Orange Blossom

The Mars Club: An erotic space adventure about mankind's first landing on Mars. The adventure begins on Earth as the candidates compete for positions on the flight team. If you think joining the Mile-High Club sounds exciting, you will definitely want to join...The Mars-Club.

The Payton Inn series: The Payton Inn is a resort hotel in Orlando, Florida. Oh, if these walls could speak, is a common phrase, and oh, the stories they could tell. Read the series and learn about the hot sexual escapades there.

Also by W.E. Sinful

The Orange Blossom Nudist Resort
Jim & Jane Become Nudist - Would You Dare to Bare? - Book 1 of the
Orange Blossom Series
The Bare Assets Band - What Would You Do for Money? - Book 3 of
the Orange Blossom Series
Debbie Wants to Go - Book 2 of the Orange Blossom Series
The Orange Blossom Nudist Resort - Would You Bear It All?
What Did You Do This Weekend?

The Payton Inn
Bachelor Party Two Different Parties Two Different Endings from the
Payton Inn Series
Birthday Present for Jeffery from the Payton Inn Series
Getting Revenge and Then Some from the Payton Inn Series - If You
Have Ever Been Cheated on You Will Want to Read about Grace and
Hudson's Revenge
Mia Goes Hooker Spotting (Includes Second Bonus Story) from the
Payton Inn Series
New Thrill Addison & Val Try Escorting
Ruby from the Payton Inn Series
Teach Me ... Teach Me Everything
The Payton Inn 12 Stories from the Payton Inn Series

Threesome - Every Mans Fantasy - From the Payton Inn Series

Standalone
The Mars Club - And You Thought the Mile-High Club Was the Club
to Join

9 798227 736048